HOW TC ᴅᴇ
AN ADULT

Funny Little Stories

By Ralph Bismargi

Drawings by

Gaëlle Baffou

http://gaellebaffou.fr

Testimonials

"The funniest book I ever read!"
- The author's 93-year-old grandfather who can no longer read.

"The writing style is extraordinary and one-of-a-kind!"
- The author's neighbor who can't speak English.

"I loved the book so much, I ate it."
- Benny... the author's dog...

Introduction

by Ralph Bismargi

His name is Jax Tyler Mann. He is 47, his body is going on 70 and his brain is going on 5.

His name is Jax Tyler Mann. Him and his wife got divorced, she got custody of the kids and he got custody of the bathroom carpet.

His name is Jax Tyler Mann. He is now happy, he is now fulfilled and his imaginary friends no longer think he's real.

True success is not necessarily about being rich and famous. It's in the little things that take us back to our basic humanity: meditating, walking in nature or pretending you are in nature with VR headsets.

When we approached JTM about publishing stories

about him, we had the hope that it would allow people to see the glass half full.

There are so many stories about successful people and pioneers - the Steve Jobs and the Oprah Winfreys of this world. But what about the people who have their coming-of-age when they're 50? Where are their authors? Where are their books?

Growing up, JTM set the bar extremely high for himself. He expected to have everything figured out from the get-go. But when he reached adulthood, JTM discovered that he was a long way from knowing it all. Life was a learning process to him. A process to improve his social skills, his professional skills and his unprofessional skills.

Table of Contents

Chapter 1

JTM's
Early Life

Earth

When JTM was in primary school, he listened when the teacher explained how the Universe was created.

He understood that there were nine planets in our solar system.

And he was disappointed to learn that these planets do not revolve around him.

JTM came down to Earth.

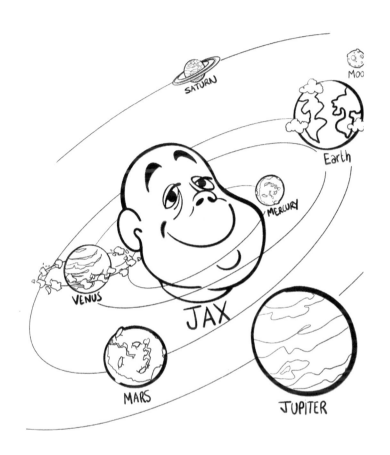

Farm

JTM's dad works in agriculture. JTM chose another field.

Growing up, JTM had to help his father with his farm during summers. Having to get up early to clean pigs with a brush was not his favorite thing in the world.

However, looking back, sour turned into sweet for JTM. Working closely with animals made him learn from a young age that they, just like humans, have feelings and emotions. They can be as good friends as humans - if not better. That is why JTM often had pets in the house as an adult and treated them like they were part of his family.

JTM also had to work with crops. Spending time in nature made him aware that every living thing has a soul and everything in life is connected. It helped him make sense of the world, make sense of life and make sense of the fluff in his bellybutton.

It was during these times of solitude that JTM felt in his heart that he was destined to do something else for a living when he grows up, but that starting out in a farm was all part of the plan.

JTM's dad wasn't expecting him to reject agriculture. The news came to him out of left field.

Siblings

JTM is his parents' favorite child. He's an only child.

Because he didn't have any siblings when he was growing up, JTM made up two best friends to keep him company: Professor John Bickerwith and Reverend Two Eyes. He would talk to them when he was alone or before going to bed every night. They would keep him company and offer him advice on whatever he was struggling with. This included how to finish his homework, how to talk to his secret crush or how to color his skin with a black marker to look like the Black Panther (his favorite superhero).

But over time, Professor John Bickerwith and Reverend Two Eyes grew up and got busy. They had less time for JTM. There was a specific incident where he had just gotten into a huge fight with his ex-wife Winter. JTM went into his bedroom and called on his friends for the first time in years. Only Reverend Two Eyes answered the call. He came and told JTM that he wanted to get back to reality and did not have time for imaginary problems. JTM got sad and decided it was time to say goodbye. He then picked up the phone and called Barney for support.

JTM's imaginary friends don't think he's real.

Standing on the Shoulder of Giants

JTM aspired to be friends with the most popular kids. He wanted to 'stand on the shoulder of giants'. But he always got the cold shoulder.

It wasn't until he had grown up that JTM made a great friend called Barney. Barney's father was an aristocrat. JTM thought he had finally found his giant. But Barney turned out to be a funny little character with long blond hair. He was the type of person who would use the flashlight from his smartphone in order to look for his smartphone.

However, over time, their friendship proved to be extremely valuable. When JTM was going through a divorce, it was Barney's support that helped him get back on his feet. From then on, Barney became

JTM's go-to person.

JTM doesn't care if you're popular or not. He just wants friends like him who are authentic, loyal and buy tennis balls just for their smell.

College

In college, JTM was torn between two majors. Majoring in math had its pluses and minuses while majoring in accounting meant he would never lose his balance.

In the end, JTM had to choose math by default because there were no open spots left for accounting. It truly was a fortunate event. JTM really enjoyed going to college because he was studying something he liked. It was also there that he met his now ex-wife Winter.

JTM is good with numbers. But it took him three months to ask Winter for hers.

Mistakes

JTM grew up thinking he was not allowed to make mistakes. But as he got older, he realized that without mistakes there would be no learning, and without learning there would be no success.

He didn't succeed on his first try when he tried to drive a motorcycle.

He didn't succeed on his first try when he tried to drive a car.

He didn't succeed on his first try when he tried to drive his mother-in-law crazy.

But in the long run, JTM succeeded in all of these things.

Fairy Tales

JTM loves fairy tales. Him and his wife got divorced and they lived happily ever after.

It all started when JTM was in college. He met Winter and they fell in love. After two years of dating, they decided to tie the knot. The years went by, their children grew up, their pets grew old and the couple grew apart. It wasn't either of their fault. They were just too young when they met and not mature enough to know that they did not belong together.

When their marriage reached its expiration date, JTM lost custody of his children, lost custody of the family umbrella but kept custody of his cervical pillows. It was a fair deal according to Winter's lawyer.

JTM is holistic. He doesn't just lose one thing. He loses everything.

Parenting

JTM always had an amazing relationship with his three children. They would let him watch TV if he finished his meal.

JTM's eldest son Jax Junior is now 20, his middle daughter Eva is 18 and his youngest daughter Ruby was a fish. When his children were born, JTM was having a quarter-life crisis and had become cynical about everything. Work and daily chores had overtaken his life. He didn't have time for himself anymore. Once they had grown up a little bit, JTM learnt from his children how to have fun and appreciate the little things in life. For instance, they taught him how to find joy in building a snowman, decorating a Christmas tree and throwing sand at strangers on the beach.

Jax Junior and Eva also learnt a lot of lessons

from their old man. They will apply these lessons for the rest of their lives. He taught them all about kindness, honesty, generosity and cleaning their ears.

Jax Junior and Eva have both left the house. JTM can now stay up as late as he wants.

Chapter 2

JTM's

People

Skills

Falling Out

JTM once had a falling out with himself.

He was late on his electricity bill and found out that he was going to be charged extra money. JTM was mad and gave himself the silent treatment for a week. Even when his own reflection in the mirror tried to reason with him, JTM wasn't having it.

Things almost got out of hand until his friend Barney tricked him into doing couples therapy with himself (JTM was initially told he was going to a piñata party).

The therapy session helped JTM understand that his relationship with himself would set the tone for all his other relationships. It also taught him how to resolve conflict in a healthy manner. Finally, it taught him that he doesn't have to dress as a piñata to go to a piñata party.

JTM is back on talking terms with JTM.

Names

JTM is really good with names. He's always giving people new ones.

When JTM was in ninth grade, a new student arrived at his school halfway through the year. The teacher officially introduced him to the whole class on the morning of his arrival. The following day, JTM had lunch with him at the cafeteria. They became good friends. Months went by, and JTM could not remember his name from the official introduction. It was too awkward to ask by that point. When he eventually had to introduce him at a party, JTM was a little nervous. He did not want to disappoint his friend after all this time. He thought he would just try to guess his name and hope for the best.

"Guys, this is my friend Patrick."

"My name is John," answered Patrick... I mean

John.

"Sorry I meant to say John. Patrick is my cousin, I just saw him earlier today. This is my friend John."

JTM does not have a cousin called Patrick but his excuse was easily accepted by John. JTM remembered the incident and thought he'd do the same if he ever forgot someone's name again.

Years later, JTM was helping an older friend buy furniture. He was filling out the delivery form for them. He got the address right, but when it came down to writing the name he got that awkward feeling again. It took him right back to middle school and he remembered what got him out of the situation back then. He went for a crapshoot and wrote "Jason" in the name field.

"My name is Susie," said JTM's mother-in-law.

"Oops, my bad. I just saw my cousin Jason earlier today and had him on my mind."

JTM slept on the couch that night.... not the one his mother-in-law had just bought.

Short

JTM is short. So is his temper.

He once snapped at the neighbor's dog for waking him up during his afternoon nap. When the neighbor tried to say something about it, JTM firmly replied:
"He started it!"

Another time, JTM lost his nerves in front of customers at work because the secretary had not put enough sugar in his coffee. The customers decided to take their business elsewhere, and JTM had half of his salary docked that month.

He learnt from that fiasco that he had to control his temper. JTM tried many anger-management techniques such as jogging, journaling and barking like a dog. None of these worked. The aha moment came when Barney told him that he usually holds his breath every time he's about to freak out.

It wasn't long before JTM had an opportunity to test this technique. He was having Sunday lunch with his wife at his in-laws' house. His father-in-law, Frank, put too much ice in JTM's soda. JTM wanted to dress Frank down in front of the entire family. Just as he was about to open his mouth, he realized he did not want to sleep on the world's ugliest couch again. He held his breath for over a minute. When everyone asked him what he was doing, he just said that he had the hiccups.

JTM's temper is short, but his breath is not.

Decisions

JTM is not scared of making big decisions, big decisions are just scared of JTM.

When his oldest son Jax Junior finished Kindergarten, JTM needed to decide whether to put him in private or public school. JTM was torn. Public school was cheaper, but his son would get more attention in private school. JTM let the decision make itself. He signed his son up simultaneously at the two schools. Only the decision never made itself and JTM paid two school tuitions for the first month. At the time, his now ex-wife, Winter, had to step up and decide that private school was the way to go.

JTM's indecisiveness was a predicament that Winter always had to deal with. JTM not being able to decide where they would go on holidays, whether they had to change apartments or what kind of chewing gum they were going to buy at the supermarket.

In his next relationship, JTM will not be scared of stepping up and making important decisions. He will choose peppermint gum.

Overreaction

When JTM was struggling to get his children to stand still for a family picture, he took his camera and smashed it. He couldn't keep things in perspective.

JTM tended to overreact to trivial things. If he accidentally bumped his toe on the leg of his bed, he would wail as if he had had lost a limb and would have to spend the rest of his life hopping around like he's playing a game of hopscotch. If a pigeon pooped on his car, it would be as if somebody shattered the car with a baseball bat, and he had to spend $25,000 to fix it.

Vice-versa, JTM used to respond casually to things that should make him jump out of his seat. When his landlord threatened to kick him out if he was late on his rent for the third time, JTM thought he wasn't serious. When he slept in his car the following week,

JTM knew that he was.

Until one day, his wife (now ex-wife) Winter lost one of his socks. JTM reacted as if she had burnt the house down. When she threatened to kick him out of the house that wasn't burning, JTM realized that maybe he had overacted a little bit... From that day on, he made an effort to keep things in perspective.

JTM no longer makes a mountain out of a peanut.

The Right Hand

When JTM was between jobs, there was an opening at the company where Alex, his brother-in-law, worked. It would have been the perfect job for JTM. When he asked Alex to pass his resume along, the exact response he got was:

"I injured my right hand, I can't pass anything along."

"Why don't you use your left hand instead?" replied Jax.

"I'm right-handed," answered Alex.

Years later, JTM was divorced and no longer speaking to his ex-wife. Alex came to JTM's house on her behalf requesting the ruby necklace that she had forgotten there.

"My right ear is hurt. I can't hear you."

"Can't you hear with your left ear?" asked Alex.

41

"I'm right-eared," answered JTM before literally shutting the door on their friendship.

Alex went back with both his right and left hand empty that day. A few days later, after a lot of thinking, JTM mailed the necklace back to his ex-wife anyway.

JTM never spoke to Winter again. He didn't want to hold a grudge.

Keeping Secrets

Every little cell in JTM's body is good at keeping secrets, except for the cells that make up his mouth.

A few years ago, his childhood friend Susie asked to speak to him privately.

"Jax, I need to tell you something but you've got to promise to keep it to yourself." said Susie in a very serious tone.

"My lips are sealed," JTM replied.

"My husband's in jail," Susie explained. "He failed to reimburse a loan he had taken out from the bank. After several warnings, they took him to court and decided to incarcerate him. I don't know what to do. I feel so ashamed. I haven't spoken to that many people about it, because I don't think they would understand. I feel so alone."

JTM sighed with compassion, looked at Susie and

said:

"Your secret's safe with me. You can talk to me whenever you want."

Two weeks later, he ran into a high school friend and accidentally mentioned Susie's secret. All of a sudden, the entire community from their high school days found out about what happened to Susie's husband. She was getting phone calls all day.

But what started as an indiscretion by JTM turned into a blessing in disguise. The high school friends got together and organized a fundraiser. They raised enough money to bail Susie's husband out and help him pay the loan back. JTM was one of the donors. Susie forgave JTM for his indiscretion but he never forgot how upset he had made her.

JTM's mouth is big, but his heart is even bigger.

Extrovert

JTM is an extrovert.

If he's at home talking on the phone, the whole building will find out that his ex-wife owes him $10,000 and that he forgot to pick-up his dry cleaning. If he's visiting his doctor, all the other patients at the clinic will hear that he has a big pimple next to his bellybutton. Even when JTM is on the phone in a public mall, he has no problem giving out his social security and credit card numbers out loud for all to hear. JTM then wonders why someone has drained his bank account.

JTM is now a quiet extrovert.

Chapter 3

JTM

and the

Material

World

Budget

JTM has a monthly budget. He spends it in two days.

When his father was at the hospital for a minor surgery, JTM wanted to lift his spirits up with a surprise. His dad always wanted to get his little farmhouse repainted but never had the time or energy for it. JTM decided to get it done at his own expense with a private company. With his father being away, it was the perfect time to do it. The repainting went very smoothly. However, once it was time to pay up, JTM realized that he was missing just a little bit of money. He had overspent that month and was unaware of it. Ironically, the only person who was able to lend him the money was his father, who was delighted to hear about the paint job. But JTM would have preferred to surprise him by showing it to him live once he got out of the hospital.

JTM now monitors his spendings, otherwise his children cannot approve his budget and give him pocket money.

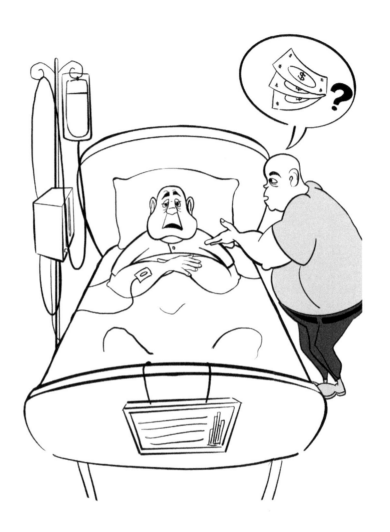

Objects

JTM does not treat women like objects. He treats objects like women.

JTM has a wonderful relationship with his phone. The first thing he used to do after waking up every morning, was say hello to it. His phone would say hello back. They would play games together, read ebooks and ask questions to their good friend Google.

But one day, JTM noticed that his phone could not cuddle, take care of him when he was sick or wear his underwear for fun. He therefore decided to spend more time with humans.

JTM will treat his next girlfriend the way he used to treat his phone.

Irony

JTM didn't understand irony. He didn't know how to iron.

JTM got to experience irony first-hand when he was dealing with his television addiction. Unfortunately, he tends to watch too much TV - more than the recommended daily intake. Planting himself on the couch and seeing the anchorman only talk to him about wars, disasters and monkeys on the loose tends to numb out his brain. The doctor therefore prescribed a one-month rehab program for JTM to de-numb his brain. Unfortunately, the program was not taught in person. It could only be followed on television. JTM therefore spent a total of thirty hours following a television-rehab program on television. It did not work. He therefore threw out his television set.

JTM later got addicted to YouTube. The doctor

prescribed a fourty-hour online-video program to help him deal with that addiction.

JTM now understands irony. He cannot get his new scissors out of its packaging because he doesn't have any scissors.

Chapter 4

JTM's
Health and
Well-Being

Going to the Doctor

JTM is 47 years old, but his body is going on 70.

Not too long ago, JTM didn't have anything to do on a Saturday morning, so he went to the doctor to have a general check-up. The doctor sent him to the lab to take a blood test. A few days later, they were both shocked at the result. JTM had an unusually high amount of cholesterol and blood-sugar levels.

"What did your previous doctor say to you when he last saw you?" asked the doctor.

"He said I had the body of a 20-year-old," replied JTM.

"When was that?"

"When I was 20."

JTM has medical check-ups a little more often now.

Emotions

JTM doesn't attend funerals. They're dead to him.

Once upon a time, JTM was afraid of negative feelings, especially sadness. He liked to keep his emotions in check. If something was bothering him, he would not allow his emotions to come out. Unfortunately it made him feel like he was trapped in a bottle.

When his grandfather passed away, JTM was devastated but did not show his true feelings to the outside world. This lasted for weeks. Until one day, everything exploded all at once.

After that ordeal, JTM realized how much better he felt for letting his emotions out and always allowed himself to openly weep if needed. He now cries if he's grieving, cries if he hears something tragic and cries if Barney got more nachos than him at the restaurant.

JTM is now comfortable going to funerals. He had to dig deep to get there.

Time

JTM lives in the present moment. When he wants something, he wants it now.

JTM never liked waiting. He could never see the benefits of slowly building something long-term.

It wasn't until he reached puberty at age thirty that JTM realized good things take time. This made him reflect on the other things he had accomplished in his life. It took him three years to graduate from high school, four years to earn his bachelor degree and ten years to get over his fear of getting on an escalator.

JTM no longer likes instant gratification. He waits a few days before popping his pimples.

Chapter 5

JTM's

Personal

Growth

Signs

JTM knows how to decipher the signs and guidance that life sends to him.

When he drives down the wrong path, life will try to tell him to change directions. He might feel bad, several of his friends might offer him the same advice and his body could crumble down like an ill-baked cookie made by his uncle Ted.

Other times, JTM may be driving down the right path. He might be feeling happy. He could be getting green lights everywhere and his spine could be tingling like a Christmas tree.

JTM always listens to what the Universe is trying to tell him. Except for this one time when he ignored the dead end sign and drove right into a giant trash bin.

JTM has a good intuition. The same cannot be said about his sight.

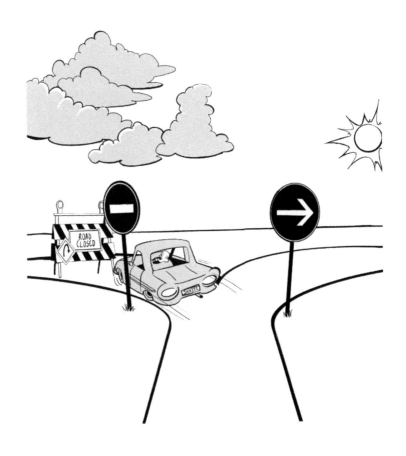

Gut Instinct

JTM knows how to trust his gut. When he has a gut feeling about something, it's because he's digesting a sandwich.

When he turned 18, JTM got his driver's license and decided to responsibly buy his own car like a grown-up - with his parents' money. It was a used Chevy.

The person he was buying it from told him that in the seven years he owned the car, it never gave him any problems. According to him, it was as good as new. JTM wanted to believe him, but something inside of him told him that this person was not being honest. He got a bad vibe and felt uneasy. But JTM ignored all of that, digested his tuna sandwich and purchased the car anyway. Two weeks later, the car broke down and his parents had to pay as much as they bought it for to repair it.

JTM now uses his gut in more ways than one.

74

The Environment

When JTM understood the impact of global warming, his heart melted.

JTM didn't believe in climate change. He noticed that summers were getting hotter each year, but he just thought he had a fever. One summer, he went to the doctor and found out he wasn't really sick.

It made JTM rethink his entire view on the subject. JTM read a lot about climate change and decided to adapt his behavior accordingly. He started recycling, used his car less often and stopped having long hot baths unless he didn't want to be the one to take out the trash.

JTM started recycling. He threw away his old habits.

Angels

JTM used to pray to his angels as if he were ordering coffee from a waiter at a café. But the waiter always got the order wrong.

When JTM noticed that he never got what he prayed for, he stopped.

'Maybe I'm asking for too much,' he thought to himself.

Instead, JTM decided to start telling his angels what he was grateful for on a daily basis. He always told them he was grateful to have a roof over his head, grateful to have loving parents and grateful to have an inflatable giraffe.

JTM also stopped asking for things and instead focused on how he could improve himself. Ironically, it was only when JTM decided to let go that his angels started bringing a lot to the table. He got a lot of pleasant and unexpected surprises that he hadn't prayed for. These included a new life partner and a soul-soothing hobby.

JTM knows how to let go. Just ask his former secretary.

Change

JTM has a lot of change in his wallet, yet nothing ever changes in his life.

JTM has had the same hairstyle for decades. Well actually he hasn't had any hair for decades. But JTM really does not like to change. He has kept the same habits and routines his entire adult life: hanging out with the same people, eating the same kind of meals and rewatching Sabrina the Teenage Witch over and over.

Until one day Barney talked him into learning something new. He decided to learn a new language: Latin. JTM dedicated himself to learning it for a whole year. Then when he decided to travel to the place where they speak Latin, he realized that, just like dinosaurs, the Latin language was extinct.

This fiasco did not deter JTM. He chose to try his

hands at something else. He started learning how to play an instrument. This time however, he made sure that his choice of instrument was not extinct before spending time on it. He chose the guitar. After a few months of practicing, he joined a choir. They invite him to jam with them once a month.

JTM made many new friends. He has a little less change in his wallet, but his life is richer now.

Chapter 6

JTM's New Relationship

Baby Food

Ever since the choir experiment, JTM became more open to trying new things. He wanted to live life on the edge. Which is why he took up a very dangerous activity: competitive baby-food eating.

When he found out that they would be giving out $10,000 to the winner, JTM quickly signed up. He followed a strict training regimen for weeks. First, he expanded his stomach by overeating, and regularly trained his jaw muscles. He also suppressed his gag reflex by training his mouth to fit as much food as possible.

Unfortunately, on the day of the competition, JTM was up against the five-time defending champion, and binge-eating phenomenon, Sandon Collins. JTM's lack of experience cost him. However, it was at the competition that he met his new girlfriend Accidental

Claudine. Ironically, she wasn't signed up for the event and had gotten there by mistake.

JTM and Accidental Claudine instantly clicked. They had a wonderful connection, a great chemistry and a common passion for inflatable animals.

The final result said that JTM lost the contest, but it didn't show what he had won: a compatible life partner that could never be bought for $10,000.

The Hairbrush

JTM does not need a hairbrush. He is hairless. But his new girlfriend needs one. She is hairful.

Accidental Claudine accidentally ruined her previous marriage through no fault of her own. She committed the unforgivable with a male coworker: she borrowed his hairbrush before a client meeting. Unfortunately, some of her colleague's blond hair got stuck on hers. When Accidental Claudine's husband asked her about the hair, she told him that she suspected she caught it from her colleague's hairbrush. Her ex-husband put two and two together, and falsely assumed that the only reason why she would be using another man's hairbrush is because she was having an affair. They got separated for a while until Accidental Claudine was able to prove the innocence of the hairbrush. But her ex-husband could not get over the incident despite couples therapy and positive hairbrush visualization techniques.

The entire ordeal turned out to have a silver lining for Accidental Claudine. She accidentally lost a husband, went through a painful break-up, but ended up finding her true soulmate later down the road.

Accidental Claudine now keeps her own hairbrush with her at all times. Unlike JTM, it is always possible for her to have a bad hair day.

Chapter 7

JTM's Career

Bragging

JTM used to brag.

When he was invited to interview for a well-paid college job at KFC, he bragged to his friends as if he had already gotten the job. It was far from being his dream job but it was the pay that attracted him the most about the opportunity. Unfortunately for him, he counted his Kentucky chickens before they had hatched. KFC chose to hire another candidate who had more experience than JTM. They put their eggs in that person's basket.

Years later, when JTM got called for a job interview at the consulting company where he currently works, he didn't tell anyone about it. Instead, he quietly studied and prepared for the interview. Even after the interview went well, he waited until he got the final answer before letting everyone know about it.

JTM was hired as a statistical consultant. This time, he didn't have egg on his face.

JTM is now humble. He brags with humility.

.

Taking Things Literally

JTM used to take things too literally. He once read that successful people don't take jobs, they create them. He therefore created a job position for himself at Dunkin Donuts.

When he was between jobs JTM wanted to make up for the job rejection he previously received from KFC. He just decided to dress up as a cook and show up for work at the kitchen at Dunkin Donuts. He told his new colleagues that he was the new recruit and started working with them making donuts as if he was part of the team.

About an hour later, the shop manager showed up and saw him. At 6'3", he stood much taller than JTM.

"Hello. Do I know you? What are you doing here?" said the manager.

"I work here," replied JTM.

"Who hired you? I'm the person in charge of recruitment here," replied the manager.

"You hired me," pretended JTM.

"I don't know you," answered the perplexed manager.

"Yes you do. We met last week and you said I could start on Monday," insisted JTM.

"No I didn't."

"Yes you did. You just forgot."

"No I didn't, please leave the premises or I'll call security," threatened the manager.

"Before you call security, can I please borrow the phone to call my wife? I forgot to put the toilet seat down this morning," said JTM to soften up the mood.

But the mood did not lighten up. The manager proceeded to grab JTM by the uniform and throw him out of the Dunkin Donut. JTM landed on his behind after flying through the exit.

JTM no longer takes things literally. Except when he took Barney's pop corn without asking him.

Deadlines

JTM loves meeting his clients. He doesn't like meeting their deadlines.

JTM once got in trouble because of that. In one specific case, he was late on delivering a huge market study to one of his company's biggest clients. As stated on the contract with the client, late delivery meant a price discount, which meant that the company lost some money. JTM missed out on a promotion because of that incident and didn't feel very good because of it.

He felt like he let the people around him down. He let his family down because he lost the opportunity for increased income. He let his managers down because they weren't sure how if they could rely on him anymore. And most of all, he let God down as he wouldn't talk to him anymore.

After falling out with God, JTM realized that he had a problem with procrastination. He kept postponing the problem but now he had to face it head on. JTM sat down with Barney to figure things out. They came up with little techniques for him to stop procrastinating. Barney was going to act like a coach. He offered to help JTM prioritize his assignments, manage his time, stay disciplined, eliminate distractions and break his tasks into little chunks of chocolate.

The techniques worked. Over time, JTM became more productive and was able to meet deadlines left and right. He finally got the promotion he rightfully deserved. God also came back into his life and joined him and Barney for drinks as the three celebrated JTM's promotion.

JTM now meets his deadlines like the French fries meet their Happy Meal.

Dream Job

JTM does not want a dream job. He wants a daydream job.

JTM has been working as a statistical consultant at the same company for over a decade. Studying graph functions has its ups and downs. Although he likes his job and is good at it, his heart tells him that there is more out there for him.

He tried to determine what he liked to do with the help of his friend Barney, but he couldn't think of anything. His mind drifted away. That's when Barney thought that he should daydream for a living. At first, JTM thought it was a joke. But then he realized that daydreaming could be fun. After careful thought and analysis, they found that the only way for you to get paid for your daydreams is to write about what you daydream and become a writer.

JTM therefore started his own blog. Since he understands all about patience, he knows that he won't be able to get paid for his daydreams straight away. His only problem now, is that when he sits down to blog, he is not sure what to blog about.

JTM would like to daydream but his mind keeps wandering.

Blog

JTM didn't know what to blog about.

He wanted to blog about the fact that he was good with numbers but something didn't add up.

He wanted to blog about practical jokes he used to play as a kid but he had a funny feeling it wouldn't be interesting.

He wanted to blog about his love for horror movies but he was afraid his blog would get ghosted.

JTM finally decided not to blog about anything in particular. He just blogged about whatever he felt like talking about when he sat down to write. Within a few months, he started getting more and more online attention.

Even though it didn't allow him to quit his job, JTM's new hobby has made him feel happy and fulfilled. Happy because he's doing something he enjoys, and fulfilled because he can finally use the word 'fulfilled' in a sentence.

Vibrations

JTM never believed in the law of attraction. He found the concept unappealing.

When he read that his vibrations were frequencies that attract things into his life, JTM's first reaction was to change the settings of his cell phone in order to change the vibrations. It didn't work.

But over the years, JTM worked on himself, learnt from his past mistakes and became good at adulthood. He gradually started feeling more content and at peace with himself. Because his inner reality attracts his external environment, JTM's hard work has finally paid off. He now has an improved career, a new passion, a healthy relationship, a healthy body and a healthy bellybutton.

If JTM can do it, so can we.

Conclusion

JTM believes that life can be fun and shouldn't always be taken seriously.

If you believe in reincarnation, just tell yourself that if you haven't learnt from your mistakes in this life, you can always come back in the next one and do better. Who knows? You might reincarnate as a beautiful butterfly, or the son of the President of the United States. Or you could come back as a mosquito, live for a month or two, and then get sprayed by an annoyed human being. Nobody knows. Just ride the wave.

JTM and his friends would like to wish you the best in all of your aspirations - self-improvement, self-development or self-underdevelopment.

Acknowledgments

by Jax[1]

Hello, this is Jax.

Jax likes to speak about himself in the third person.

He cannot speak in the first person because he's got his imaginary friend Professor John Bickerwith with him all the time. He also cannot speak in the second person because he's got his other imaginary friend, Reverend Two Eyes, who comes to visit every now and then. Finally, he cannot speak about himself in the fourth person because that would be plain delusional.

Jax would like to thank himself as well as the author for writing stories about him and sharing them to the world.

Sources

1. Acknowledgments Section - All material in this section has come from Jax's fictional brain (2020)

2. No other source was used in this book (2020)

A Note from the Author

Thank you so much for taking the time out of your busy schedule to read my book.

The idea for HOW TO BE AN ADULT initially came to me when I was filming an episode of my web series in 2017. In that episode, the main character, Herbie, is reading a fictional book about how to ruin his life. When we were done editing the episode a few weeks later, I thought about actually writing this fictional book but never had the time to sit down and do it.

Over a year later, I was taking a short break from the corporate world and finally found some free time to write. After several drafts, I realized that the title HOW TO BE AN ADULT was funnier and more appropriate for the character of Jax aka. JTM.

I would really like to know what you all think of this book, so please do not hesitate to leave a review. Reviews are also very helpful to authors because they allow us to attract more readers and bring you more stories.

Finally, if you're on social media, you can follow me on Instagram or like my page on Facebook.

Thanks again and happy reading!

Ralph

About the author

Ralph Bismargi is a writer, producer and director from Paris. He has traveled and lived across four continents. This exposed him to different cultures and allowed him to be fluent in four languages. Having initially earned a degree in International Business, it was his desire to explore hobbies outside the corporate world that led to his true calling. Inspired by his teachers in writing and acting, Ralph decided to dedicate himself to the arts of writing and filmmaking by listening to and learning from his mentors.

His first writing experience came at Second City Chicago where he took an intensive Comedy Writing course. A Professional Screenwriting certificate from UCLA would soon follow. To date he has produced six comedy films - including BIRTH DAY and HERBIE. His web series, INSPIRATIONAL THERAPY, earned him a great following on YouTube and many film festival selections. Ralph also focuses on writing feature-length screenplays and fiction. He has many upcoming novels and short stories on the way. Stay tuned for more updates!

You might also enjoy

Ralph Bismargi

SUCKER KISS

A Funny Short Story

Jill is a talented film director. She is filming her first TV sitcom and, for the first time in her career, there is a live audience. Her entire life is riding on this particular project. However, she struggles when a quirky audience member doesn't know how to laugh normally. Will she succeed at keeping everything together?

Trish is a talented and beautiful young actress. In order to prepare for a career-defining audition, she signs up for a new acting class. The teacher of that class is quirky Larry. Has Trish finally found a good teacher in Larry? Will teaching be Larry's hidden talent? Or is Trish going to regret taking the class?

Copyright Information

malware in the products they offer for free.) Your support to the author's rights is very appreciated and makes it possible for the author to continue producing new material to his readers.

Cover by Marie Piquemal

Drawings by Gaëlle Baffou

ISBN: 978-2-9571080-1-5

Printed in Great Britain
by Amazon

23791335R00078